PEEF
and his
BEST FRIEND

by Tom Hegg
illustrated by Warren Hanson

Waldman House Press, Inc.

To Ms. Bobbie Tonkin, teacher of all my first grade buddies,
and Nathan and Mathew Orner, my next-door neighbors.
T.H.

To Patty, my Best Friend.
W.H.

Library of Congress Cataloging-in-Publication Data
Hegg, Tom.
    Peef and his best friend / by Tom Hegg ; illustrated
by Warren Hanson.
        p.   cm.
    Summary: Peef the bear is left behind when his best
friend goes to school, but when the boy tries to become
popular by not being himself, Peef understands and com-
forts him.
    ISBN 0-931674-49-2 (alk. paper)
    [1. Best friends–Fiction. 2. Friendship–Fiction.
3. Popularity–Fiction. 4. Teddy bears–Fiction. 5. Stories in
rhyme.] I. Hanson, Warren, ill. II. Title.
PZ8.3.H398 Pg 2001
[E]–dc21   2001026263

Waldman House Press, Inc.
525 North Third Street
Minneapolis, Minnesota 55401

The day was just the kind of day that never ought to end
For Peef, the multicolored teddy bear, and his Best Friend.

They had their favorite breakfast, and they played their favorite games,

And walked the secret path they knew as well as their own names.

Why, anything is possible when morning skies are blue

And summer warms the air and high adventure calls to you.

They felt the earth begin to shake… and heard a rolling sound…

As if a thousand kettle drums were pounding all around.

A mad stampede was coming! Dinosaurs of every size

Were running from Tyrannosaurus Rex with piercing cries!

Oh, how could they escape, Dear Children? Would this mean the end

For Peef, the multicolored teddy bear, and his Best Friend?

"Quick! Grab this vine and swing!" said Peef as rows of T.Rex teeth

Were snapping at them fiercely only inches underneath.

A mother pterodactyl swooped… and flew them to her nest…

And next to her colossal eggs, the panting pair could rest.

"It's time for lunch, you two. Come in. Remember – wash your hands."

"Okay, Mom," said Peef's Buddy. "Peef – the Mother Ship commands.

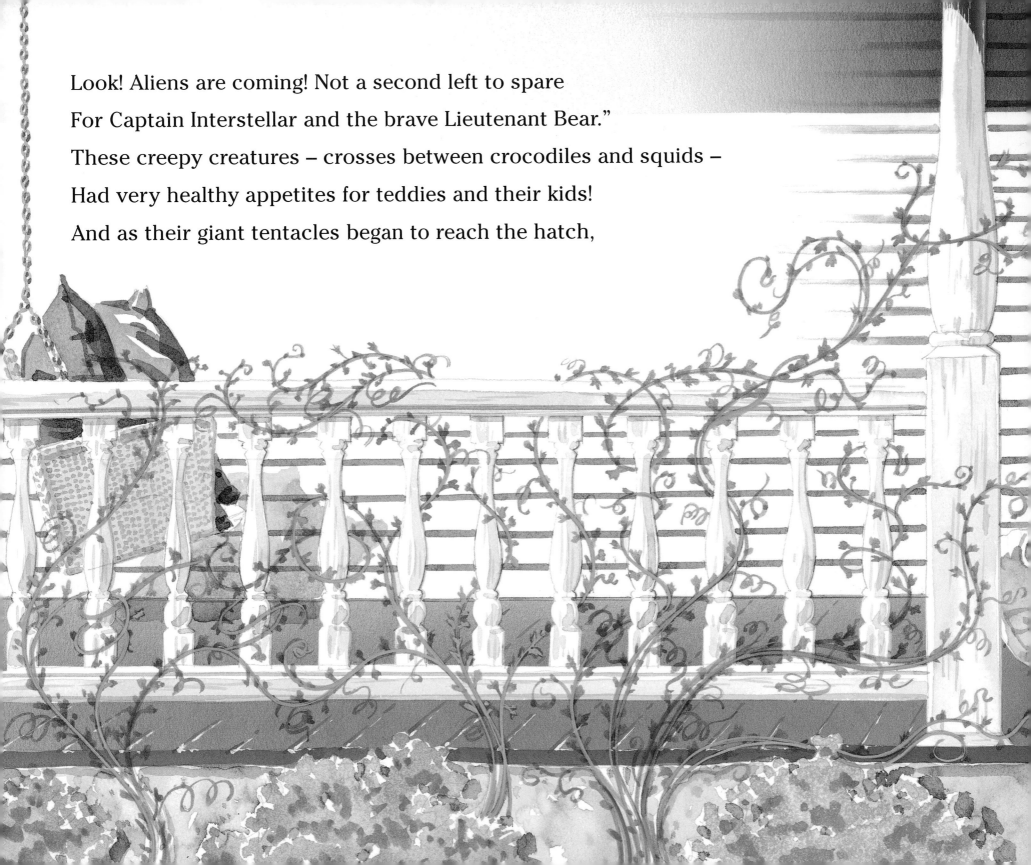

Look! Aliens are coming! Not a second left to spare

For Captain Interstellar and the brave Lieutenant Bear."

These creepy creatures – crosses between crocodiles and squids –

Had very healthy appetites for teddies and their kids!

And as their giant tentacles began to reach the hatch,

Our heroes rocketed away without a single scratch.

"Slow down!" said Mom. "Please sit and eat your sandwich. Drink your milk."

"Okay, Mom… over," said the Captain. "Peef – let's hit the silk."

They parachuted into port to take on fresh supplies,

And as they ate their PBJ's they looked around for spies.

Suspicious-looking characters were walking to and fro,

Exchanging winks and switching cases.

"Okay, Peef... let's go!"

The Secret Agents grabbed one from the tall man with the scar.

They raced through guarded hallways, out the door and to their car.

Oh, no! It had been stolen!

There were bad guys on their tail.

They grabbed a motorcycle…

and they took a dusty trail.

They bounced upon the saddle.

Bandit bikes were screaming near!

"Oh, yikes, Peef! See them coming?

Let's ske-daddle out of here!"

The bridge was out. They had to jump – it was the only way.

"Ka-Whoompf!" They ramped up in the air, their tires spitting clay…

"Ka-Runch!" They landed on the other ledge... the gorge so wide
The stinkers chickened out and idled on the other side.

"It's time to take your bath," called Mom. "The water's nice and warm."

"We're coming," said the Agent, "… and she went down in a storm.

So Pirate Cove," said Peef's Best Friend, "is right where we should be."

They got into their scuba gear and dove into the sea.

A shining school of angel fish was darting left and right.

The coral reef and Peef had matching colors in the light.

The sunken ship lay down below… and in her private hold,

According to the legend, was a chest of pirate gold!

With flippers flipping eagerly, they gained the ancient hulk…

And then, a ghastly "Yo-ho-ho!" arose within her bulk.

Complete with peg leg, cutlass and a patch upon his eye,

The Ghost of Captain Crossbones, with a water-chilling cry,

Attacked with a harpoon – and then, to man the rusty guns,

Awakened from their sleep, his trusty crew of skeletons!

"You two – get out right now. You're splashing water on the floor.

Enough time in the tub."

"Oh, please – a couple minutes more?"

Said Peef's Best Buddy.

"Well – alright," said Mom. "But this time, try

and please remember – pull the plug.

And don't forget to dry."

At last, they had to say goodnight
and climb the squeaking stairs
And brush their teeth,
turn out the light,
and say their bedtime prayers.

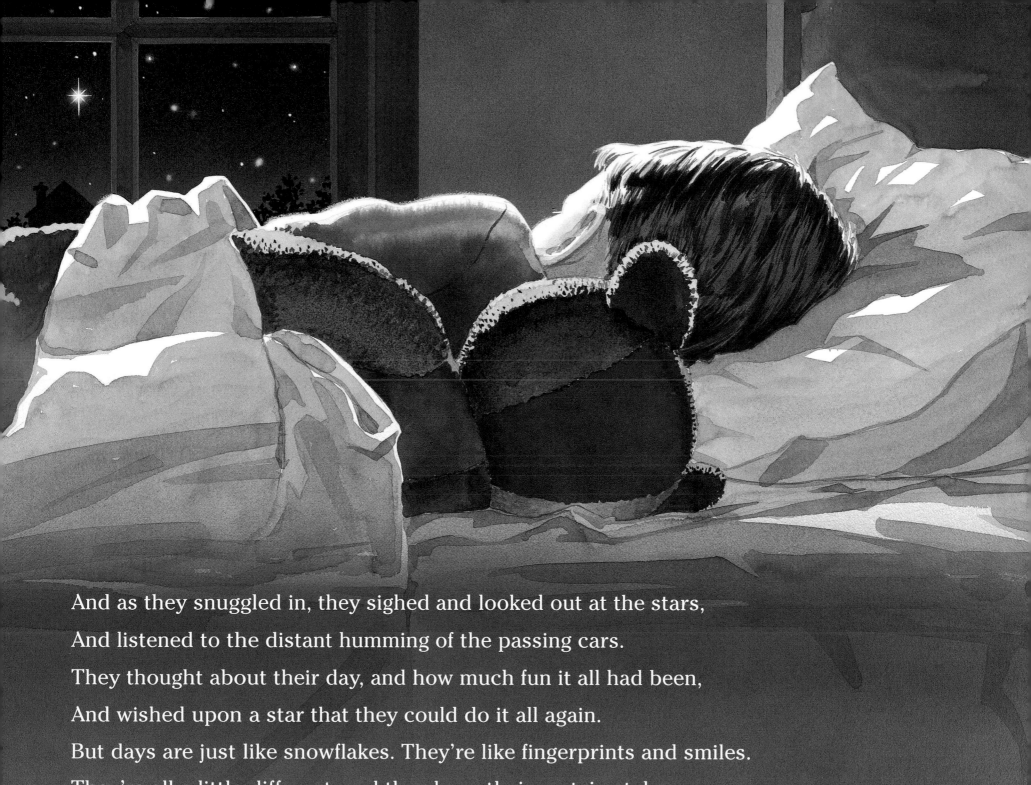

And as they snuggled in, they sighed and looked out at the stars,

And listened to the distant humming of the passing cars.

They thought about their day, and how much fun it all had been,

And wished upon a star that they could do it all again.

But days are just like snowflakes. They're like fingerprints and smiles.

They're all a little different, and they have their certain styles.

So Peef and his Best Friend had many days of summer fun,

But each was wonderful because it was the only one.

And then, before they knew it, all the leaves upon the trees

Began to color brightly and to dance upon the breeze.

Then, back-to-school shopping –
buying paper by the stack,
And picking out the clothes you like,
but putting some right back
And getting what is "sensible" instead to Mom and Dad –
(who said they went to school,
although you'd think they never had.)

Then, Peef began to hear about some kids… a special bunch

that everyone was longing to be sitting with at lunch.

"I tried to make them like me.

I'm not good enough, I guess,"

Peef's Friend began to say

because of weeks of no success.

And Peef said back, "I know that there is nothing wrong with you.
Just be yourself, and do what you believe is right to do."

Then, once upon a Friday, Peef had breakfast with his Friend

And watched the yellow school bus disappear around the bend.

Then Mom took Peef upstairs – and as she carried him, she said,

"You two are quite a pair." And then she sat him on the bed.

And then, as all good teddies do, Peef waited through the day

And thought of his Best Friend, and of the time when they could play.

At last, the bus pulled up again. The door hissed open wide,

And voices called, "Goodbye! Goodbye!" and someone came inside.

But more than just one pair of feet came pounding up the stairs.

"And this is my room," said Peef's Friend.

A new voice said, "Who cares?

Boy, you must be a baby. Look at all this baby stuff."

"I'm not," Peef's Friend shot back.

"You're not? You sure have got enough.

Hey – check this teddy bear!"
A hand grabbed Peef
and held him high.
"Oh – that.
My Mom just stuck it there.
I really don't know why.
Let's go," Peef's Friend said quickly.
"Let's not hang around in here."
"Okay. This junk is boring,"
said the new voice, with a sneer.

The hand threw Peef away.
He landed face down on the floor.
His Best Friend in the world ran out
and swiftly shut the door.

The little room was dark and still… the colors gone to gray…

And spilling from the windowsill, the sounds of kids at play.

And Peef began to cry a pool of multicolored tears.

The only thing a loyal teddy ever really fears

Had happened. How can cloth and stuffing be in so much pain?

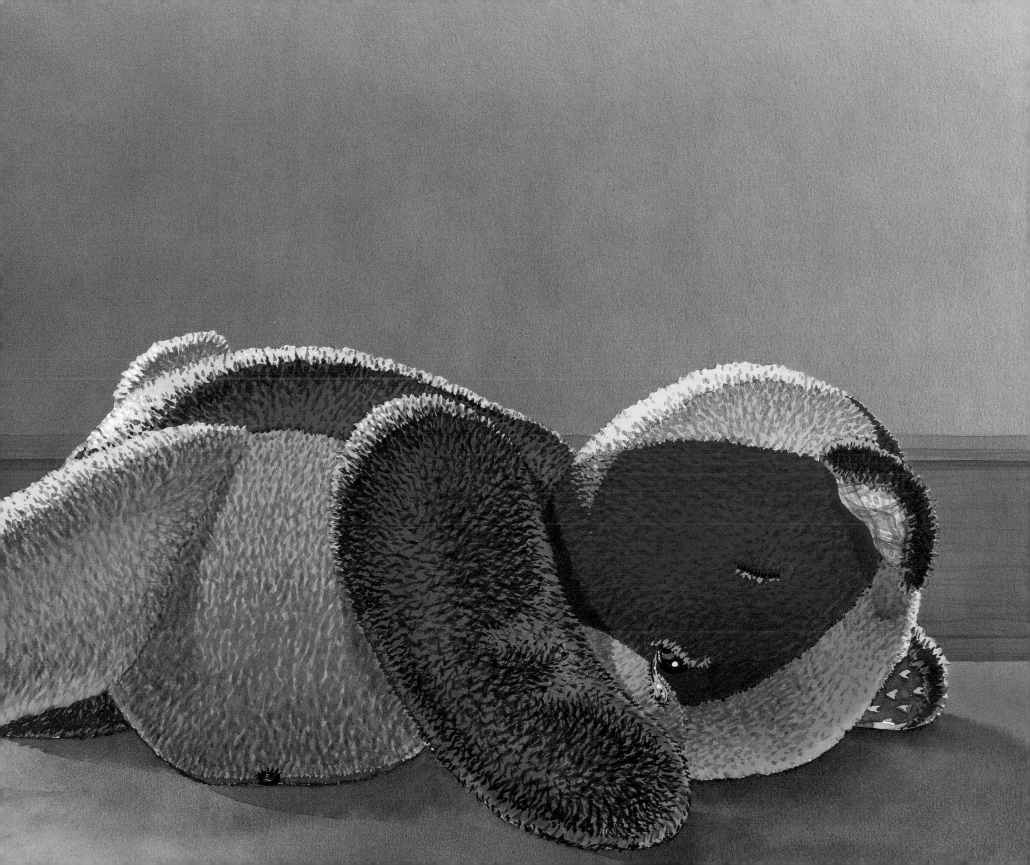

That's why I want to know – if anybody can explain –

About what happened next with Peef and his Best Friend. Two feet

Came slowly up the squeaking stairs and stood, in sad defeat,

Before the wooden door… and then, a hand went to the knob

And turned it round and pushed, as if it were the hardest job a hand could do…

And then a wedge of light came through the door
And fell upon the teddy who had fallen to the floor.

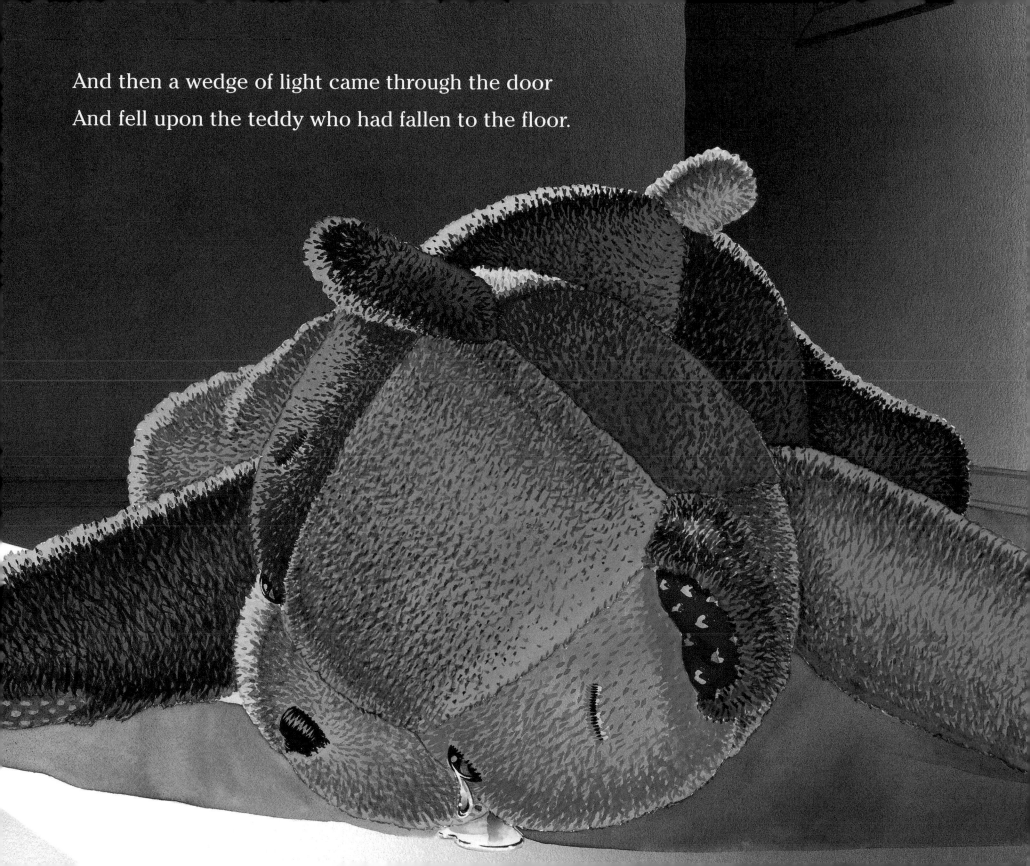

The hand reached out to pick him up…

but stayed there in the air…

And then, a breaking voice said,

"Peef… I'm sorry…"

to the bear.

Could three words be enough, Dear Children?
Would this mean the end
For Peef, the multicolored teddy bear,
and his Best Friend?

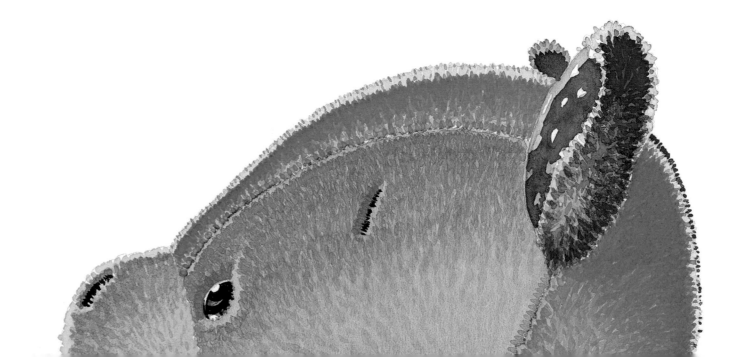

Before they knew it, they were in a cuddle and a hug

As close as any huddle in the middle of the rug.

And Peef, who has a way with words he doesn't even say,

Looked at his Friend, and silently, he said, "I know the way

You've wanted kids like that to like you… that is why you did

Whatever you could do to make it happen. You're a kid.

You acted like a person that you're not, because it seems

That being someone else might be the answer to your dreams.

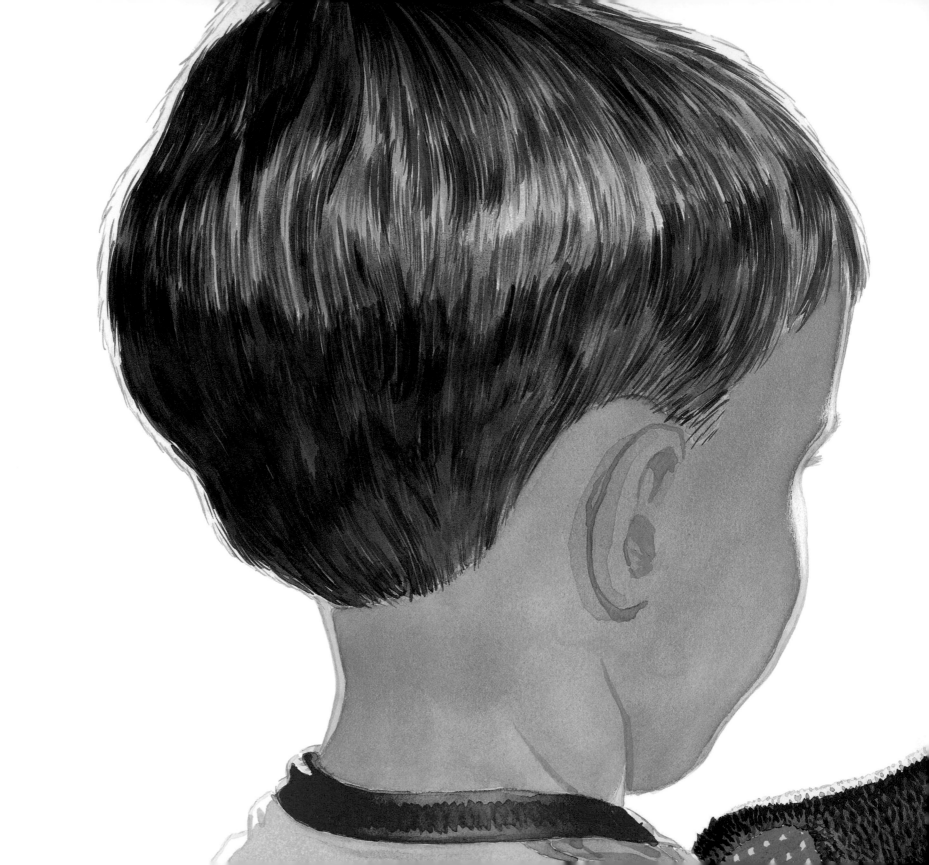

I know that you're afraid that things can never be the same
Between the two of us because of all the hurt and shame.
But no… the only thing that really hurts a teddy bear
Is when his Friend does something wrong and doesn't even care.
And even when I feared that I was being thrown away,
It didn't hurt a bit compared to thinking you'd betray
The most important part of you.
Your greatest gift by far –
No matter how it seems –
is being true to who you are.
And yes… one day the two of us
may have to say goodbye.
But when the time has really come,
you'll know… and so will I.

But now, there still are spies on motorcycles in the land.

Those dinosaurs and aliens are getting out of hand.

And there is pirate treasure to be found, and games to play,

And new adventures calling us each new and different day."

The two Best Friends got up.

They smiled and let go of their cares.

They brushed their teeth,

turned out the light,

and said their bedtime prayers.

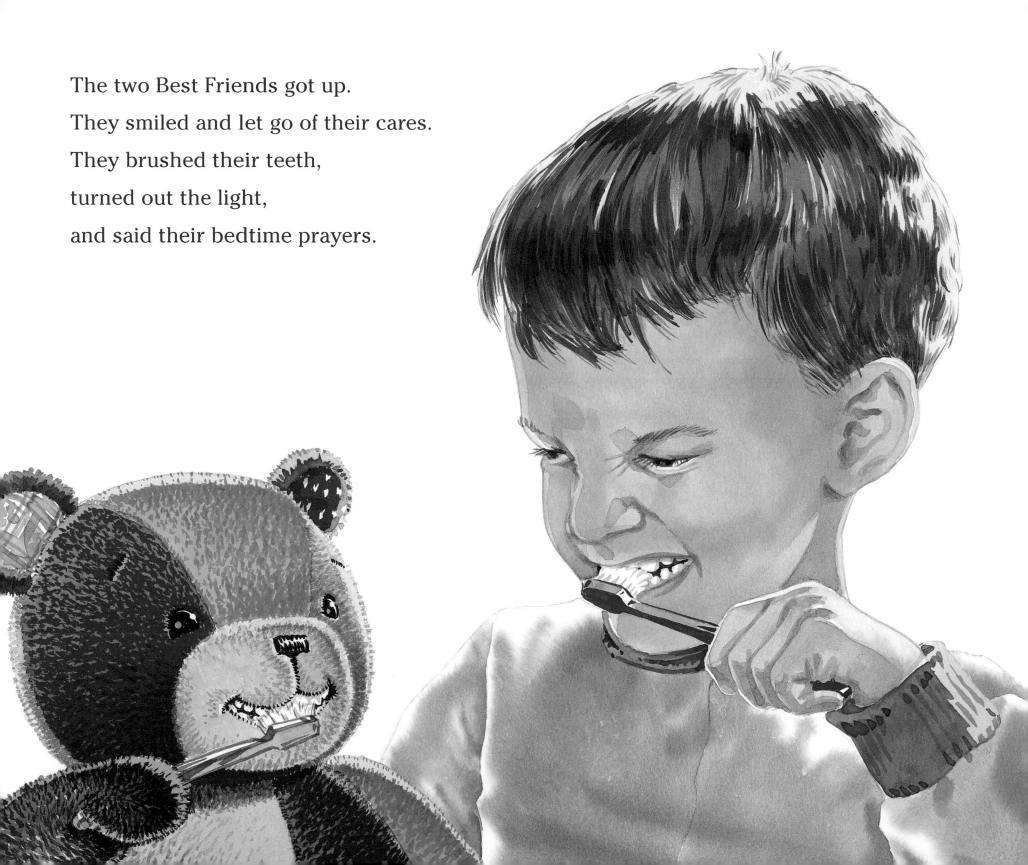

And as they snuggled in, they sighed and looked out at the stars…
And listened to the distant humming of the passing cars.
They thought about tomorrow, and the fun that lay in store,
And wished upon a star that there would always be one more.

They thought about colossal eggs… of crocodiles and squids…
Of snowflakes, fingerprints and smiles, and teddy bears and kids…
Of shining schools of angel fish beside a coral reef…

And as they drifted off to sleep, a little bear said, "Peef."